To Caleb –

Evie Finds Her Family Tree

All the best,
Ashley B Ransburg
2009

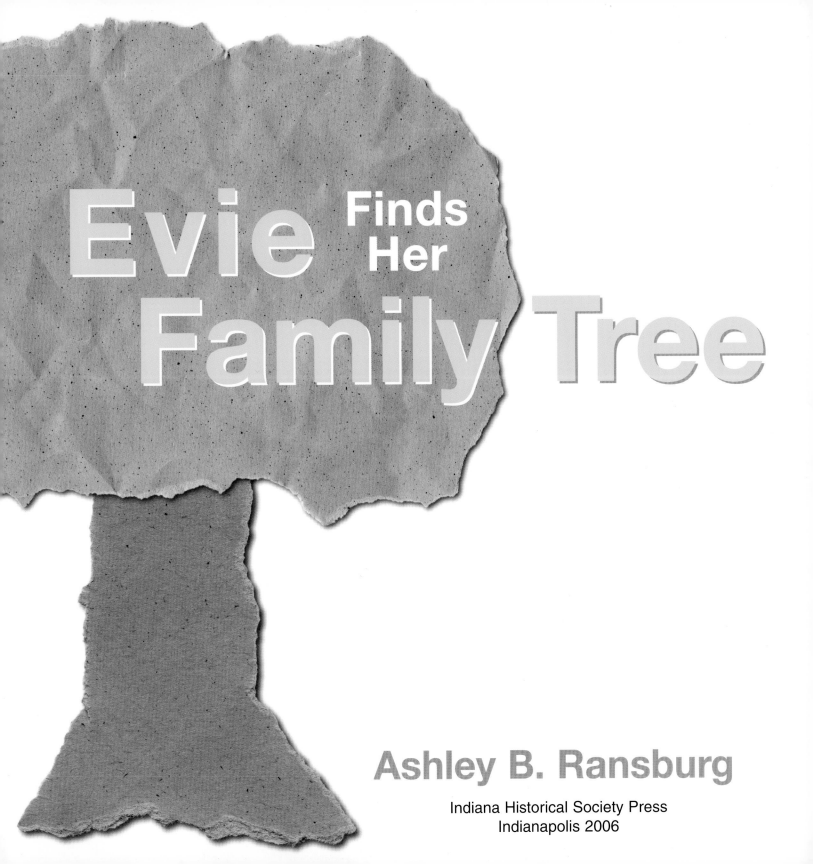

Evie Finds Her Family Tree

Ashley B. Ransburg

Indiana Historical Society Press
Indianapolis 2006

© 2006 Indiana Historical Society. All rights reserved.
This book is a publication of the
Indiana Historical Society Press
450 West Ohio Street
Indianapolis, Indiana 46202-3269 USA
www.indianahistory.org
Telephone orders 1-800-447-1830
Fax orders 317-234-0562
Online orders @ shop.indianahistory.org

Library of Congress Cataloging-in-Publication Data

Ransburg, Ashley B.
    Evie Finds Her Family Tree / written and illustrated by Ashley B. Ransburg
      p. cm.
    Summary: When Evie overhears her parents talking about their family tree,
      she considers whether they mean the holly, the sugar maple, the magnolia,
      or the oak.
    ISBN 0-87195-187-8 (alk. paper)
      [1. Trees—Fiction. 2. Family—Fiction.] I. Title.

PZ7.R173Evi 2006
[E]—dc22

                                                        2005049287

Printed in China

To everyone on my family tree,
with love.

Evie was just about to fall asleep when she heard her mom and dad say something about a family tree.

"I wonder what tree is *our* family tree," Evie thought to herself.

When Evie woke up in the morning the first thing she saw was the holly tree just outside her bedroom window.

On a snowy, winter day, Evie loved to watch the deer come from the woods behind her house and eat the berries.

"Maybe this is the family tree Mom and Dad were talking about," she thought.

The holly tree sure did remind Evie of her dad. His whiskers always tickled her cheek as he gave her a kiss goodnight.

"And Mom always laughs because they tickle her, too."

"But not everyone in my family is just like Dad, so I better go find a different tree."

Evie ran to the front yard where she found the magnolia tree. Even though it was far away from the house, the sweet fragrance of its blossoms always caught spring breezes and found its way inside.

"Maybe this is the family tree Mom and Dad were talking about," she thought.

The magnolia tree sure did remind Evie of her mom. Evie always knew when her mom was about to come into the room because her perfume got there before she did.

"And my little sister always plugs her nose because sometimes Mom wears too much perfume."

"But not everyone in my
family is just like Mom, so
I better go find a different tree."

Out by the fence line in back of the house, Evie spotted the maple tree. She liked to sit under the maple tree with her mom on a summer day and read a book in its shade. They used the seed helicopters that fell from the tree as bookmarks when they went in the house to get a snack.

"Maybe this is the family tree Mom and Dad were talking about," she thought.

The maple tree sure did remind Evie of her little sister. Whenever anyone asked her sister how old she was, she held up her hand to show her five fingers pointing straight into the air. Her hand looked just like the marks that damp maple leaves left on the front sidewalk.

"And Dad always chuckles because she is really only four."

"But not everyone in my family is just like my little sister, so I better go find a different tree."

Evie skipped over to the big oak tree in the backyard. In the fall, she loved to reach up to the low branches and help the squirrels collect acorns for the winter.

"Maybe this is the family tree Mom and Dad were talking about," she thought.

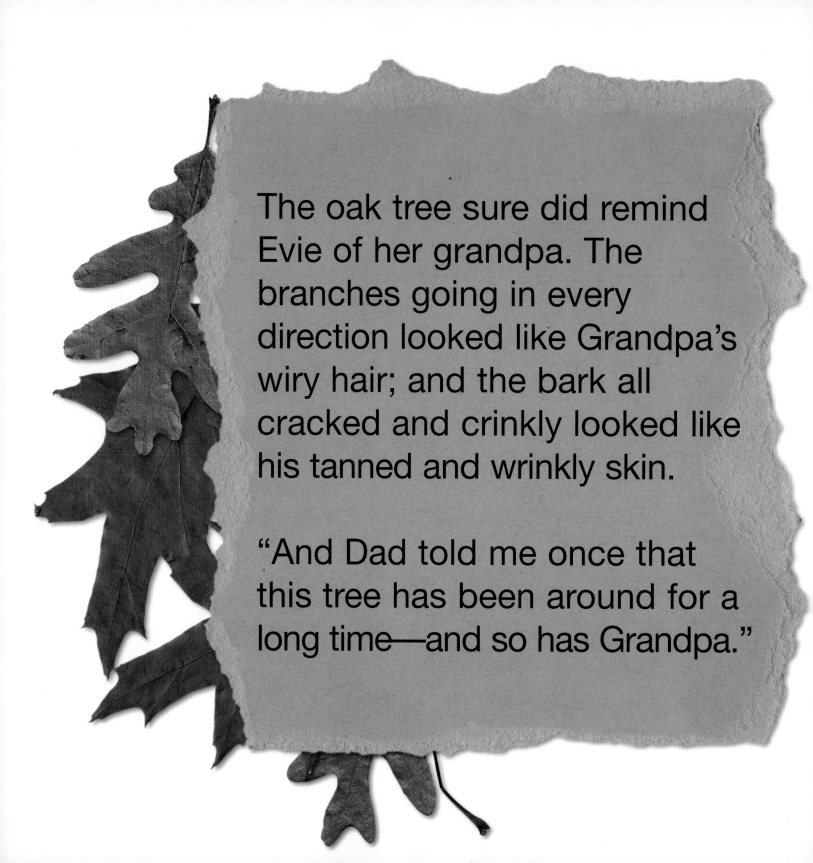

The oak tree sure did remind Evie of her grandpa. The branches going in every direction looked like Grandpa's wiry hair; and the bark all cracked and crinkly looked like his tanned and wrinkly skin.

"And Dad told me once that this tree has been around for a long time—and so has Grandpa."

"But not everyone in my family is just like Grandpa, so I better go find a different tree."

But as Evie looked around, she realized there were no more trees in her yard.

"So what tree *is* our family tree?" she wondered.

And then she got an idea!

Quickly,
Evie
grabbed
an oak
leaf,

then she ran back
to the maple to
get one of its
leaves, too.

She circled the house
and snatched a
magnolia leaf,

and she ran to the holly tree
to gather a few leaves from
its branches.

When Evie saw all the leaves together, she finally found what she had been looking for.

Evie found the tree her mom and dad had been talking about. Her family tree! It was made of parts of everyone she loved.

And Evie smiled because she knew it was her tree, too.

**Many thanks and much appreciation
to the gardeners of this tree:**

Sally Grant
Julie Enyeart
Catherine Bennett
Teresa Baer
Paula Corpuz
Judith McMullen
The Hendrickson Family
Julianna Short
Laurie Durham
Katie Georgene
Shelby & Ryan Jasper
Cheryl Ransburg

and to the sunshine:
My dad, Gary

You can find out more about your family tree by reading these books:

For Children

Baer, M. Teresa, and Kathleen M. Breen, eds. *Finding Indiana Ancestors*. 4th ed. Indianapolis: Indiana Historical Society Press, 2000.

Hasler, Brian. Illustrated by Angela M. Gouge. *Casper and Catherine Move to America: An Immigrant Family's Adventures, 1849–1850*. Indianapolis: Indiana Historical Society Press, 2003.

Sweeney, Joan. Illustrated by Annette Cable. *Me and My Family Tree*. New York: Crown Publishers, 1999.

For Adults

Baer, M. Teresa, Kathleen M. Breen, and Judith Q. McMullen, eds. *Finding Indiana Ancestors: A Guide to Genealogy Research for Hoosier Descendants*. Indianapolis: Indiana Historical Society Press, 2006.

Morgan, George G. *How to Do Everything with Your Genealogy*. New York: McGraw-Hill / Osborne, 2004.

Renick, Barbara. *Genealogy 101: How to Trace Your Family's History and Heritage*. Nashville: Rutledge Hill Press, 2003.

To purchase additional posters or books on the Web, go to:

shop.indianahistory.org
or
EvieFindsHerFamilyTree.com